ENOKI

THE DARKEST SEA

ENOKI

ANNA.M.L

Published by

THE DARKEST SEA

www.thedarkestsea.com

ISBN: 978-0-6456741-0-1

First published 2023

Cover design by ANNA.M.L

Artwork illustrations by ANNA.M.L

ENOKI images are copyright © ANNA.M.L. All rights reserved.

Preface

noki had slipped. A small stone had wedged between her ribs. As she shifted, the snap of twigs beneath her let out shrieks like sparks. Earthen debris scattered from her dress as she pulled herself up.

Behind her was a rock face from which she had fallen. It held a deep steep curve like a wave. She travelled its escarpment with her eyes. It was long and wide. Its steep incline barred any attempt at return. A wall impossible to ride.

A forest wrapped right along its perimeter. She walked along the edge to look for an exit. After about half a mile she stopped. There appeared no end. With no advance and no retreat, she turned to the forest.

In front of her, a mangled arrangement of leafy overgrowth marked its entry. Dark and foreboding.

Maybe she should stay in the safety of daylight, she thought. But to stay was to starve.

Enoki looked left, then she looked right. Then she looked ahead. With wide eyes she stepped forward into the forest.

ENOKI

Chapter 1

A gnarled bough breached the barrier between light and dark as though desperate in its twisted wreckage to find the sky. Enoki followed it in traipsing its roots. Why then was she going in, she thought. Because in must be the way out. The scent of bark, mud and leaves had more life. Behind her was nothing. Nothing but a trap for foraging coyotes.

Shards of light broke through the leafy membrane above. It lit the way through a winding alley of trees. It looked like a thoroughfare. There, she thought, must be a way out to the other side. As she walked towards it, her foot stubbed the edge of a protruding root hurling her forwards. She braced her trip with her hands slapping the bark of a tree. It stung like sandpaper. It was enough to detract from the small throb in her rib whose pulse was fading.

Indentations like the skin of a lizard marked her palms. She lowered her hands and walked on, this time carefully inspecting each footfall. She didn't know how long she would last without any shoes. But the ground beneath was soft and moist between the sticks and stones. The soles of her feet would get used to it. She told herself to keep going.

As she curved around trunks and collapsed branches, the density of the forest enclosed her. It was matched by an increasing echo of amphibians and larking birdlife the deeper she walked in. The drumbeat of crickets clicked en-masse. Its prominence amassed a confusion. But it was no chorus of embrace. There was too much coolness in the air. The sound was like a chain being pulled fast. She could feel the pull of its tide. Movement was its antidote. To continue and go along, rather than restrain against it.

Privet shot up between woody conifers, as creeper vines strangled a willow up ahead like a tourniquet. Pretty weeds sprung up in grass-like shoots. Suckers projected from the base of trunks like tassels among saplings that joined a procession like a fleet eager to exploit their green sails. It was a gentle wind that rocked them from their anchor point. Their low lying brush concealed all paths. The thickness of their foliage marked a sense of impenetrability. The grey bark of a beech tree illumined a green grey from the reflection.

Enoki moved her arms in front of her to sweep past the sprigs. A tiny cricket jolted like a spring from leaf to leaf in front of her as though in a lily pad dash on a pond. How many of these leaves held insects on their undersides was a thought Enoki had to swiftly expel. She just stepped forward into the scrub with her arms the first combatant, a pantomime of averting spider webs in the night.

The sound of clicking insects wreaked a heavy bedlam. In the distance she could see the swift darts of finch-like birds fling themselves across a corridor, like paper balls flung from windows. So too whose sound rung through the forest air.

The unison of activity was like witnessing a parade or protest down a long laneway flanked by liquid amber. But this was no festivity nor dissent. This was a demonstration of the habitat into which Enoki had

stepped. But it was the length of the corridor of trees that Enoki could see, when she stretched on her toes, that daunted. See too much and you get more than you bargained for. Clearness of view had a certain reality that overwhelmed. Remaining foot down with a leafy veil protected and concealed the longitude into which Enoki had stepped. All she knew was to move forward.

She entered a dense cloister. The ground started to feel colder and damp as she moved through the scrub. The air subtly delivered a moistness to her nose and a scent reminiscent of rain on concrete until it became a pungent wet bark. Amphibian life rang louder. It sounded and felt like water was nearby.

Up ahead a stream gurgled past a broken trunk. She skipped over pebbles and straddled fallen branches and waved past concaving ferns in eagerness looking for its salvation. With the stream at her feet, she'd found manna. She leant down and cupped her hand into its icy cold water, filling it to the brim. Tipping it into her mouth, it quenched her thirst relieving the dryness of her throat. At least there was water. Water to survive. That's how they did, she said to herself as she inspected the ferns and branches for birds. She sat on the edge of a stone and washed the dirt from her feet.

From the corner of her eye, in the distance, she thought she saw a snake slink itself up along a fallen branch. She picked herself up, ready to run, until a closer look revealed it was just a curved piece of bark. The panic it brought eclipsed the relief. She decided to keep moving. She headed well clear of the mistaken reptile. This trick was enough to make her want to turn back. But that's all it was. A mistake of the eye. There was no turning back.

She flicked aside stringy shoots from saplings and overhanging branches. Ferns that dangled in concealment, grazed on passing. Their wilted veils she learned to bypass. After hours of relentless slices and scratches against her bare arms, the streams of light through the thick growth started to fade. Daylight above was closing. A coming darkness

dictated her only choice was to stop for nightfall.

A nearby tree housed a wedge of roots close to its trunk encased by a bed of leaves. This would have to do. It was dry enough to rest on. She slunk in between like a cat in a cubby hole. The air was still enough to not be cold. She smoothed out the creases of her dress surrounding her knees and thighs. Night shadow concealed the hazy dust upon its fabric. She gripped around her dress-clad knees in some form of reverse will to wrap its cloth about her like a sheet.

She was sure she could last through this night, as a fog descended blanketing all within.

Chapter 2

A soft flutter tickled the side of Enoki's cheek. She opened her eyes and then closed them. She thought she was dreaming. The flutter made its way to her arm. She brushed her arm in a half doze. The tickle returned like a feather on bare skin. She dozily opened her eyes. What appeared perched on her arm was a giant moth. Startled she leapt up from her slumber and flicked it off. The moth shot up and danced about Enoki's face. She flapped her arms trying to shoo him away. He landed on her head. She could feel his weight and flicked at the strands of her hair trying to get him off. The moth flew off and landed on the bark of a tree. Enoki leaned back, rattled by this provocation. The moth was dead still. Enoki leaned forward, now curious to inspect this creature that had disturbed her sleep.

He had large bulging eyes an opalescent black.

More like a cross between a fly and a moth. But this *was* a moth. His wings were a glistening black down like a raven with the stripes of a tiger, silvery when caught by the light. His midnight colour stood out from the bark of this tree. He'd be camouflaged closer to the blackened hollow. He was so still. Was he waiting for her to make the first move? After all the fuss around her face, now he had decided to play dead. But Enoki couldn't help the feeling of being inspected by those eyes. She tilted her head at him, seeing if he would flinch.

A splinter of morning light harshly struck through the trees hitting the bark. The moth dashed off his perch and seemed to disappear.

Well, that's that then, Enoki mulled. She looked around to gain her bearings. A mild confusion grasped her. It hadn't been a dream. Being in this forest. She really was here in a forest. She looked around through the wayward trees, curled around so many would-be paths.

13

Enoki expelled a tired breath at the prospect of what she'd begun. Of what was ahead. This way or that. Which way had she come when she waded in the dark. She looked to a garlanded path. This was the path she decided to tread. There wasn't much choice.

A few steps under its crown Enoki felt a familiar flutter and weight upon her. She turned her head around. The moth was back. He had landed on the back of her shoulder. She flicked him off again with her hand, quickening her steps to outpace him. He just returned, skirting the strands of her long hair. She dashed out a huff of annoyance. Can't you find something else to cling to, she expelled.

She stooped as she thundered forward, as though tasked with carrying a bundle she didn't want. He stayed there, on the back of her shoulder. The more she walked on, the more he stayed. She was a free ride, she thought. This must be the right direction, though, she told herself, otherwise he would have flown off in a direction of his choosing. She could feel herself straighten. This must be the right way.

Creeping vines, twisted stringy bark, collapsed branches adorned with withering leaves encased this path. Enoki skirted boulders and sidestepped potholes of mud. She looked down at her feet. They were already filthy. Yes, this is the right way, she asserted. She trudged and thudded through this wood.

There was only one way as the thicket around her increased. It was like walking through a cave. She was sure it must already be midday. But the stole of ferns and leaves had turned it to midnight. Those small medallions could create such blackness when they wanted to. Searching for some sun, trapping everything beneath them, suppressing attempts to be there first. A race to the light.

The darkness started to suppress. Enoki ducked down a crack between wilted ferns in the hope it might be a tunnel to some light. On hands and knees she scrambled through the overgrowth. It overwhelmed in its length, metastasising the further she crawled. She dragged across rough patches and felt her knees skid through mud. Bits of twig poked at her back that made her quicken to a dash. She started to panic. Maybe she'd gone too far to nowhere. She sucked in the air that was thickening. Its moistness had suddenly become suffocating. She felt a pain in her chest like a spike. Enoki dashed forward. Now she wanted to get out.

She dug her fingers into the ground, clawing her way as fast as she could. She could feel the sting to her knees as she fumbled over grit. Dashing through the thicket, she finally broke through its tunnel, shuffling through its exit to a wide opening of trees.

Her heart raced in a propulsion of beats as she stood up slightly off balance. She let out a breath, then collapsed beside a rock feeling a sting in her fingertips.

Her nails were encrusted in dirt. One had a split that stung like a bee and was encased in blood. She wrapped her hand around it, hoping its pressure would stop its painful throb. Her knees were raw like a pomegranate skin. She had a sudden feeling of wanting to cry. Where have I gone?

But no tears fell from Enoki with the ebony eyes. When feeling returned to her body, she became conscious of a presence. The moth had clung on. He was still there on her shoulder.

Then it started to rain.

ENOKI

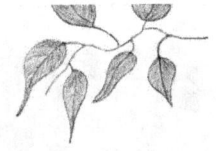

Chapter 3

Droplets pattered through the canopy. It was a slow moving tap dance upon the drum skins of a thousand leaves. Enoki looked up as drops sliced down from above and started to wet her skin. There was no time to refrain to wonder at its subtle entrance. All things small could grow to things big, she knew. She needed to find a hollow.

The opening of trees she sat among offered no shelter. It was heavily surrounded by dense foliage. She ducked her head under a wedge of leafy overgrowth and shimmied underneath, crouching in awkward steps tunnelling through its encasement of brush.

A twisted trunk caught her eye in the distance. She quickly moved toward it and ducked down between a small cavity between the earth and its undergarment of bark, wedging herself underneath.

All Enoki could do was sit and watch as pellets of rain skipped off leaves and hit the ground in front of her, hoping it would soon pass.

With its tap, tap, tap, the soft slaps on leaves and smell of wet earth unlocked a fresh sapling sweetness. It filled her head with a clearness. It felt clean to breathe in. A calm had descended that slowed her beating heart. A slowing of time to reset.

She fingered through her hair that had become knotted and damp. Her split fingernail stung, so she just let her hair go, a tangle of waves. What did it matter. No-one was here to see her in the rain.

Like thoughts to untangle, sometimes they should be left for a clean breeze in a blue sky. She was sure she would find that blue. But didn't she just leave a blue sky behind? Ah, yes, but what she wanted was a cerulean blue.

The moth had relieved her shoulder and flapped to the curving awning of the trunk. He flicked his wings to dispel raindrops scattering it like a fine mist. His coat silvered in the wet and light. Enoki stared at the moth, unsure of this companion. Maybe he'd be gone by the time it stopped raining. A strangeness dodged at her at the hope he would not. Wishing upon a moth. She was suddenly panged with a laugh and a cry. She looked away from the insect in a daze, along with the thoughts to dispossess. She

could feel her eyelids heavying and a desire to doze. The day had been long. It tired in this twisted maze. Never-ending paths and corners and curves. Before long she fell asleep.

To sleep with the rain was like a walk through a daydream. Afloat upon a sea where each wave scattered its droplet mist upon the deck of a tiny vessel. Its wooden drumming beat a hesitant rhythm. Its sound providing strange comfort, like a damp cloth on wet skin. It roused and consoled. With heaviness it could alarm like a flogging sail. Until the sound stops. Here she was upon a sea of dead leaves.

When Enoki awoke it was the black of night. Grey light marked shadows by a dim moon. The depth of field disappeared. She suddenly couldn't remember where she was. Gaining bearings in the dark was near impossible. Then she remembered. She was plunged with a sick feeling of not knowing what to do. Should she just stay where she was. The rain had stopped. But the ground was cold and damp. She just sank further into the hollow. She survived last night. Now she'd hit repeat. The marching beat that pumped her through the last two days was eclipsed by night time crickets and frogs knocking at the drum of her ear with a profound intensity. I'll just stay, she thought. No use, I can't see in this dark.

The night passed, followed by another. And another. Days seemed long the more she trudged over roots, staring at a forever cluster of trees like a fistful of straw, hoping to find the long one that was the right curved path. Whereby around that curve was the sun. An exit. The sooner she rounded a curve, all it led to was a curling frond to beat away.

She changed her point of view to above. Way up high she could see bats fly. If only I could get that high to see a border, she thought. It was a perspective beyond her. Its vertigo lashed. The force of thoughts in pursuit of an escape stifled Enoki's momentum. She closed her eyes.

If she could see in her mind's eye an unambiguous trail, then from the ball of her foot she'd depart this point with the force of a falcon in free flight, no longer a bird left static by its manacle.

She opened her eyes. Looking up she could see the moon in the break of the canopy. It was fractured by razor-like shards of sticks. Maybe it was a reflection of a broken dream. Something too remote then hacked at by an angry artist's marks.

But the moon was a light and lit up the trees. An owl was perched in the crook of a branch a little off in the distance. It appeared the owl was looking in her direction, solid at his post. Secretly regal, his white feathers softly glowed.

Owls were not a predator to her, she thought. Though he didn't stop his inspection. The owl's head had stopped at a fixed pose, like a wooden nesting doll, but you couldn't reach to twist open the layers to see what was encased within. A wisdom trapped in his chest. She withdrew behind a tree, uncertain of this creature's point of view.

Stay on this path. Keep going. She focused forward. A cluster of blackberries hung from a bush, their black skins radiated a dark blue hue in the moonlight. She plucked a few and savoured their tart sweetness. She hadn't eaten for days.

ENOKI

Chapter 4

It was the early hours of the morning. Enoki watched as a small squirrel snatched an acorn from the ground in front of her. He fled in haste out of sight whisking behind a tree. She wondered what little cavern he called home. A place for his foraged wares within which no other foot could tread. Did he have a little door to his hollow to shield himself from intruders?

Two parrots bolted between trees in the distance, fast like bullets in their chase. When their day's race closed, maybe they shared the same tree, nesting one above another, high up and hidden. A place where no-one could view, so no-one knew their private conversation when they chose to bundle together within the one nest. Too high to hear. Too high to see.

She pulled at a stem close to her feet. Twilling it

between her fingers gave off a scent of camphor. Here she was wedged in a vista between an oak and a laurel. To dismantle her languor she picked herself up and made way.

Up ahead there were tendrils like tinsel wrapped around branches, until closer inspection revealed their thorns. As she walked underneath their adornment she stepped on a prickle. She stopped and picked its spike out of her sole. Here, there was no cotton wool. She straightened her dress and her shoulders. A few pricks were no reason to cease. She walked on.

As she progressed past clumps of low-lying ferns at the base of trunks, she saw what she thought was a mole with his head sticking out of his burrow. He seemed to notice her, or perhaps not on account of his short sight. He stopped still as she passed. She wondered what he hid in his underground. Despite his earthen den, his burrow would be his and his alone.

Here in this forest Enoki had nowhere to burrow. Nowhere to conceal herself from this forever outside. The forest had a notion of a roof with the trunks as its walls, but inside its mass cocoon was a place of constant exposure, where Enoki shared her shell with every other thing under its canopy. But perhaps that was its deception. These woods had no walls. If you can't see the walls, there was no within them. Only within walls was a private abode. There was no door behind her to close. No architrave upon which it could attach.

This trail in Enoki's forest was shared without want. But with the moth on her shoulder, his constant return upon it seemed to acknowledge either an approval of her direction or in solidarity of her predicament. If only she could interpret its anomaly.

To go left, to go straight, to backtrack and curve right, what did it matter. At least she was moving. Thrust amidst an insect and animal gaze. This forest was a sea with a giant swell. It hid you in a dip and exposed on a crest. She could stay low and move with a rhythm in step with the landscape view. Clusters of heavy bush were the dip and clearings were the crest. It was a confused perspective. Heavy bush suffocated and a clearing was the fresh air. The landscape was to be an obstacle no matter the course. She proceeded with a determined force and carried herself forward.

The day progressed and as with each step over untouched ground, Enoki pressed into its unacquainted dominion. As her body pushed through each invisible boundary, she breached its vacuum exposing it to human eyes. Nature revealed its flurry of activity by day and its rush hour as light began to fade. It wound down in human parallel.

The dusk was completely still. No breeze brushed through the twilight air. The soft sounds of crickets grazed through the sky as birds made haste for their nests calling out their song of soon to be rest. Enoki could feel the stillness upon her skin, around her being. It was like a condensed chamber, a miniature habitat within a cloche. As a bird darted to somewhere, it had a presence that projected confident pursuit. All Enoki could do was but stare out into its wilderness.

Chapter 5

The moth skipped along the air behind Enoki as she walked through the wood. When she stopped, he stopped. When she continued, he pursued. It tantalised and distracted. It comforted and annoyed. All Enoki could do was walk on with him.

She walked through a section of pines. The moth dashed from trunk to trunk to her shoulder in a hopscotch frenzy, darting between its needles in a depiction of play or possibly prowess. It left her harried and oddly amused. She wondered if he ever tired. If he'd had a belly big enough or gills like a fish, could she see him panting through his effort. The answer was upon her shoulder where he always seemed to return. This was his moment of rest. She carried him forward as she walked on.

Late afternoon had struck like a cold blow from

an arm sledging a rosy hue. The wood was to reveal its unnerving arena. A tree emerged in Enoki's line of sight with spikes like a medieval armour. It thwarted her passage with its potential for carnage. Then something on it halted her completely. She beat back in refrain. Some type of reptile had found it a home for its camouflage. It was the bat of his eyes that had him sprung. Then he let out a deep bellied growl.

It was like he was waiting on a signpost to monitor and deter her passage. She momentarily froze. Enoki felt a creeping feeling of inspection by these animals she'd pass. The forest dragon snapped his eye at her from his spikey vertical column. Like a spy with a camera solely directed upon her. She moved left. His eye followed.

What do you want? She yelled. Why are you spying on me for? She lashed out.

For all the hours of conversation Enoki had not had, herein lay her only discourse – from provocation. A provocation that turns animals into sentient beings. Enoki just had the need to speak and expel as though someone was there. She knew she was likely a predator to this dragon. As soon as she lurched forward he fled. So much for the scaly skin and thorn-like horns exuding from its back. He was frightened of her. Like the scale on a fish skin,

you scrape hard enough it comes off. An animal can make you fear him if he wants to. But beneath his layers is just another body protecting himself. A dragon was no different from a skink, except for the insulation of his size. Nevertheless she'd avoid his path.

She made her way quietly to the side. As she skirted the blood-letting tree her heavy tread transformed to a light one. Tender were the soles of her feet despite their dirt. But her skin was thickening. If she trod on the dragon, maybe he would be the injured.

Up ahead two more reptiles appeared stuck like magnets to a lichen covered tree semi camouflaged by its moss. Again they held their gaze on Enoki. One let out a slow growling hiss. She lurched forward again. This time they didn't flee. Enoki expelled a breath in contempt. She leant down and picked up a rock. When she stood up they were gone. If only she had a pocket, she thought. She let the rock fall from her hand. It was then she was reminded of the only weight she was carrying. The moth was there on her shoulder – still. She turned her head gently and peered down to him. Maybe it is you they want, she said softly to the moth.

Enoki carefully stepped onward. She knew a

lizard would not be her only confrontation. They hid and evaded and like any animal they could attack. Defending one's territory can have its valour, but it has its avarice for a place in common. Enoki had a right of passage in this forest, as any one of the animals. We were all of some organism. But the shape shifting cell transformed according to its place of birth. This tower of trees was a place of cunning. Enoki was yet to be baptised.

The days turned to weeks. There was no relief. Her body ached. Her ankles and legs cast with a hundred scratches. Sleep at night was scarce. When her eyelids were closed, her ears remained open. She could feel a pressure in her head that wouldn't abate. Too many half nights, too much looking down, troubling where she walked. Too much of a forest hanging over her. This forest was not her friend.

Too many eyes peering in, watching, waiting, spying and gossiping, not helping. Little eyes peering between the leaves like tiny tots hiding behind table cloths hoping not to be caught in the cracks.

A small furry animal hung on a branch, curling its fingers above her. As it made haste and jumped to a higher branch, she realised she was at the foot of a fig. Scattered on the ground were scores of its fruit. She knelt down and picked up a bulbous form. She lifted it to her nose and could smell a subtle sweetness through its skin, until she pierced its side with her nail, its aroma more profound. Then she sunk her teeth in. It was the largest fruit she had found for all the days she had been here. It was exotic. It filled her with a sugar that would power her for days.

Relieved of her hunger, she stretched her arms above her head like in a salute to the sun. It relieved the strain of the passing threat. She breathed in the spirit of continuance. She had to keep on going. If fruit of the forest was like a four leaf clover, how many would she be lucky to find. Their scarcity governed their legend. Her find proved their existence. Despite the desire to stay and consume and possess their sugar, she turned and looked ahead. She knew could survive.

Chapter 6

With a new day she set off in vigour, striking aside the shoots of green, snapped twigs as she trampled, crushing leaves in grit. As she moved ahead, she waved away foliage under the never-ending canopy until her steps wearied and her arms hung heavy. No matter the strength of the last few days, the bleakness of Enoki's surrounds was oppressive. It hung like a heavy curtain Enoki didn't have the strength to pull back. When she looked ahead all she could see were vines strangling tree after tree in a long distance repetition like a room of mirrors. If only she could push one over so they dominoed, falling like pictures on a deck of cards, not real solid timber impossible to shift.

But in this dark room, there was a reprieve. The only delicate constant. It was the moth. He was still with her. As she sat to regain her strength he flew to a collapsed log and perched on its tip. She got on her hands and knees to a crawl then lay on the ground in front of him and just stared. Why had this odd creature followed her all this time?

Why do you follow me for? She asked out loud. She stared at his opal eyes, curious how this creature rested so serene, staring straight back at her. If only you could help get me out of here, she said. If only you were human.

Enoki stared longer resting her chin on her hands. There was stillness in his silence. It made her aware of the other noises, subtle in their insertion into this quiet. But the silence of the moth was like a line of communing only with her. No conversation required. Another who knew she was here.

Enoki rolled onto her back and stared up at the breaks in the trees revealing the slithers of sky. Small birds sped from outpost to outpost darting like flicking tongues. A dragonfly hovered up to her right, spying like a drone upon her and the moth. The moth was solid, unphased. She didn't know who usurped the other in this forest. The dragonfly continued to hover before resting on the edge of a branch. Enoki rolled back to her belly and turned to the moth.

You have a friend, she said.

She wondered what the rules of engagement

were among the insects of the forest. Such inter-dalliances were only for food. Who fed whom, she pondered. Who laid the feast for the others.

The dragonfly flew away.

Enoki stared at the moth. He continue to stare back. There was something about his eyes. Like there was something he wanted to say. All he could do was just be there on the broken branch in front of her. If you weren't here, there'd be no-one, she thought. No-one to be here with me.

Clusters of leaves dangled and shuffled from a subtle breeze like ladies waving handkerchiefs to a boat departing its dock. Like they were saying goodbye to words.

But the absence of words brought back the foreboding of her surrounds. Enoki pushed herself up. If she wanted out she had to keep going. As she stood up and walked ahead, the moth flew up and fluttered to the back of her shoulder. There he relaxed his wings. Upon her he seemed to have found his home.

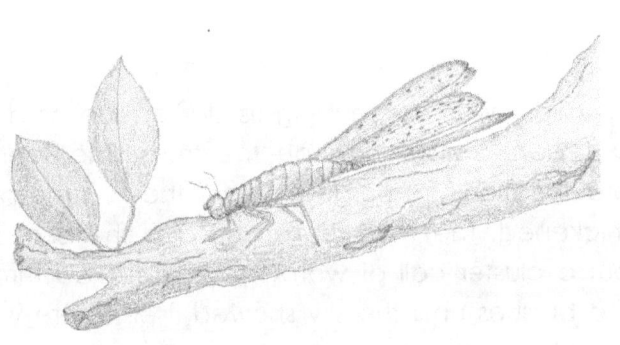

Chapter 7

Twilight was descending its darker hue as a swift breeze swirled through the trees. The scent of precipitation emerged as the atmosphere thickened. The wind picked up and the birds rang out a cluster call of warning. Enoki flicked through the brushes until the sky showed itself. There was a coming storm.

Charcoal tumbled curves through the sky. Three starlings sprinted ahead of her with piercing shrieks. Enoki's heart jolted in fright as her eyes darted around to look for a refuge. The pines started to twirl like slow moving hoops. The cluster of treetops in the distance shuffled into a frenzy until their leafy shards split off haphazardly into the air. Like a coming wave, the wind suddenly caught her, whipping around her dress.

Twigs flung from their branches and leaves

projected like splinters in Enoki's path. The force of the wind had become strong. She pressed forward, pushing against this angry monster's breath, covering her face with her arms.

As she forged forward, the force of the wind made each step as though through mud. She waved her arms to fight back debris that shot forth like glass.

The humidity clashed with an icy sleet above cracking a propulsion of thunder like a hundred boulders tumbling down a mountain. As the sleet pricked her skin, with squinted eyes, Enoki groped to a large toppled tree trunk, ducking into its cavity. She swept away strands of hair from her cheeks.

As she squatted underneath, she could see within a few feet a bird jumping up and down on the ground, letting out harried tweets. The bird was jumping around a small clump on the ground before it. As the bird dashed and squawked around it revealed its frenzy. Its companion was dead. Enoki could see the frenzied bird's tiny eyes blink from the sprinkle of rain, its feathers speckled wet, clumped upon its small brow. Its beak slowed to a small cry. The bird's jumps depressed themselves until it stopped still. It emitted one last silent cry, then flew away, leaving the tiny feathered clump behind.

Maybe it had been a mother bird crying over its

fledgling, fallen from a tree, not strong enough to fly back to its nest. Maybe it was a lovebird, unable to save its beloved. Maybe it was a sibling unable to protect its twin. Maybe it was a father crying over a fallen son.

The fallen bird was small. Its demise made Enoki feel smaller. Enoki who was crouching under a giant fallen tree that had collapsed in a mammoth forest up against a tumultuous force of nature bigger than any of them. Nature dictated mortality. It also enacted perpetual tests.

When nature enacted an angry power, the survivalist enacts a tact beyond his feathered down or shirt on his back. Enoki wrapped her dress down harder around her knees, down to her feet. I'm too small, she thought. There is too much of 'it' and not enough of me. Her line of sight was marred by a bird, already frozen by the rain, broken by the wind.

Enoki coiled back her dress and ducked out from under the trunk. She reached for the bird, clutched it up in her hand and returned to the trunk, placing the lifeless form underneath. Here is where you will lay, she said. The moth dashed up in a ring around her.

Enoki pulled herself away from the trunk and rushed through the wood, with the moth trailing behind her, haphazardly tugged by the wind.

Hurtling twigs and leaves sprayed around as Enoki pushed on in the only path visible. Her hair flew back with the forging wind. The sound of animal life had vanished.

I must, she said. I am stronger than you, she yelled to the storm.

She groped against the wind and spitting rain, straining to see in front of her. She slid down a short hill before tumbling down a rocky embankment. She moved too fast and her feet slid on a mossy slime. The smooth rock was slippery, wet from rain. In an instant she plunged into a pool of water beneath the boulder.

The shock of the cold stung as she shrieked underneath. She darted up to the surface in half gasps of air, gulping in water. She raised her arms up along the boulder but couldn't get a grip. It was too large and slippery. The cold made her muscles freeze adding a heaviness to her labour. Her head without want sank back under the surface. This water hole was deep. Her feet could not touch the bottom. With a propulsion of her legs she kicked her way to the surface once more. Again she scrambled her arms up another boulder. The effort failed itself, as she collapsed back in the pool. She could feel her jaw clench in cold. Pain gripped her everywhere.

She tried to search in the dimming light, where

she could see a small cove. There she waded to a lower collection of rocks. She moved her arms slowly, grabbing upon the rocks and pulled up feeling the weight of her body. She wedged her foot into a gap and pushed herself up and out.

Exhausted she crawled upon a boulder away from the water hole and slumped her body face down upon it. She was too shattered to move, as she closed her eyes, pale and drained, breathing slowly in the cold.

An hour passed as she lay unmoved. The wind gust in swirls above her. In that moment she was oblivious.

In a half daze, the storm's thrash made Enoki come to. She slowly opened her eyes as though from a deep sleep. Splinters of rain cut at her skin. She knew she had to get up and move. Her teeth started to chatter as she shivered. Cold to the bone she pushed herself up with her hands looking around for a shelter.

A cluster of boulders housed what appeared to be a small cave, tucked into the side of a hill, from what she could make out in the darkness. A muffled sound of water interspersed among the thrash of wind ripping leaves.

Enoki glided into the cavernous space. She immediately felt its relief. She curled into a corner, feeling the iciness upon her skin and pain of her tendons. All her muscles ached. She closed her eyes. Upon opening them again, she reached to the back of her shoulder. No. He wasn't there. The moth had gone. She was panged with a feeling of dread. A descent into nothingness. Abandoned in the cold.

The room was so dark she needn't close her eyes again. Her skin was so numb, she needn't feel for anything again. As the storm bashed its weight outside upon stone, all Enoki could hear was the sound of running water.

*

In the early hours of morning, a light peeked in. The air outside was still. Enoki could see a fine mist just outside from where she had housed herself in the cave. She crawled out to find a waterfall up and to the right of the cave's opening that had been the source of the waterhole. Its mist cast spirals at its base. The scene before her was in picturesque contrast to the night before. If you had not been there you would not have known there was any storm. The light was muted, but enough to reflect off leaves and wet rocks and illuminate this cove.

The waterfall cascaded from a short cliff with

dense foliage and rock either side of it. A small hill covered in a down of moss was where Enoki had slid. She walked to the edge of its plunge pool, cupped her hand to drink. She could feel it's effervescence upon her face.

She raised her hand to feel the back of her shoulder. Deprived of its constant, it delivered a sadness at the night's truth. He was gone. Lost to the storm. She looked about upon the hill and the rocks and roots. There was nothing to find. No tiger-like stripes to spot. A loss that made her lose her breath. In desolation, she turned back to the pool before her.

The pool of water trickled off in a stream. If only she could read its ripples like tealeaves at the base of a cup. Enoki wasn't sure if she should follow the stream or climb back up to the top. Life was usually at the end of a stream, not up the top. Streams were where there were people.

She stood up and stared at the waterfall. But streams led down to nothing but a hole, harder to get out of. Enoki climbed over the rocky embankment making her way back up to the top.

As she reached the peak it showed a flat clearing before another collection of cedars and pines. A mass of vine appeared to have half untangled from atop, withering forlornly, evocative of the affair of

ENOKI

the night.

Enoki walked through it, as she pulled down a strand of its curling hair to clear the path revealing more dense forest ahead. It housed a path cradled with fallen branches. Remnants of the affair of the night were visible in the darker cloisters, where the wind broke it from above. The only way through was over and under all the tangle of branches. An obstacle of ruin.

ENOKI

Chapter 8

Enoki straddled a log and skirted upended roots. As her foot struck the edge of an object, she was suddenly projected forwards. Unable to stop her trajectory, she curled and fell to her hands and knees. Her eyes widened in fright and her heart jolted. Her mouth fell agape as she sucked in her breath. In a panicked frenzy, she surveyed behind her. She thought she'd struck some animal.

The quickening of her pulse hesitated into a slowed beat. She rested on her knees. There was nothing but a stalk and mangled roots. But in the moment of quiet a sudden rustle was heard in the bush. Provocation of there being an animal pricked her consciousness.

A more profound thought dogged her. What if there were another person? Enoki cast aside these intrusions. She knew she was alone here. She could feel it. Isolation has a scent only its inhabitants know. Enoki knew this jungle was hers. Nobody else was here. No-one human.

She didn't know if she should run. This trip had stopped her still. Again she heard the rustle in the bush. This was not a place to rest. It was a place to depart.

Enoki looked about to see if there were any animals. Anything that might move, that made a sound. But the constant ringing of amphibians and insects clicked through the air. It masked the movement of any other form. As she stood up from the ground, she was the loudest sound.

She gently stepped away. With her eyes locked to the side, she viewed an opening of foliage that looked like a trail out. She ducked her body through its passage.

With each step came a disconcerting quiver. A trailing of something behind. She looked behind. There was nothing there. On she walked. But she could sense a tug like a string being pulled behind her, like a vine had cuffed to her ankle like a leash and the remains of a ghost she left behind decided he wanted to follow. She stopped and turned around. Nothing. She looked from her knees to her heels. Nothing. She turned forward and walked ahead.

A rustling accompanied her steps, like something gliding through dried leaves on sand. It became more prominent. She stopped and with the slightest turn of her head she gazed back. She gasped with a ping in her chest as snakes counting three emerged behind her. They slithered in a twirling motion in her direction.

With an electrifying propulsion she sprinted forward, sucking in the air with each footfall. Like a hurdler on a track she jumped logs and swooped over brushwood swiping the sprigs that scratched her skin. She needn't look back, the snakes were relentless. Their hiss and slither were audible in their chase and pricked Enoki's ears, provoking her to run faster. She ran harder.

She grabbed a fallen branch of pine needles on the run and threw it behind her sure it would stifle their path. She continued to dash forward. She jumped up a twisted bough and climbed a trunk certain no snake could trespass. It could be an enclave of safety until they passed, finding another piece of prey.

With heart pounding, out of breath, she looked down from her perch. If they could see where she went at least they couldn't reach, she thought. There at the base they slithered.

Be off, you devils, she yelled. Why can't you prey

on something else, she commanded.

Enoki's scent must have been like a mouse to a cat. Thought of as easy meat. I'm not easy, Enoki knew.

Hours passed. The reptiles slithered out of view, like dispossessed sycophants denied entry.

As Enoki relaxed against the trunk, sitting in the wedge of a branch, she realised it was the first time she had climbed so high. It was a haven away from the rot at the roots. No wonder the birds made it their home. But she was no winged creature able to fly off to the next perch to make headway, to find a way out. Enoki was a ground dweller. Her only headway was upon sticks and stones. Unlike an insect ready to pounce.

Animals had a sense beyond any humans. The vibration of the ground, the flutter of a leaf, the scent of sweat in the distance. Only human calculation was what she possessed. She could only go with what she knew. I know I can't stay here. The risk was in her taking.

She descended down the trunk of the tree in trepidation and cunning, gently easing herself from the bough. She tenderly clung on as she stepped her foot to the ground to detect if her footstep on earth would arouse a re-emergence of wrath.

ENOKI

She let go and slipped her body out and through to the other side of the path. It was another trail. Maybe this would be her escape.

Chapter 9

Days had passed. Fronds and saplings had started to diminish. Leaves seemed few. Maybe the seasons were changing. The air was cold and dry, not thick. Enoki was walking into a stack of brown and grey. Like a winter wood that forgot its snow.

Enoki could see three bats picking at bunches of red berries from a branch up high. They appeared to be eating them, leaving the spoils like confetti on the ground. Enoki was starved. She'd had no food for days. She carefully approached the tree from where the bats and berries were hanging. She plucked up one of the branches that had fallen to the ground. It was encased with a cluster of berries. The bats beat out a chipper as she took the bunch. It startled her at first. They must have been fruit bats.

She took one berry to her mouth and nibbled

ENOKI

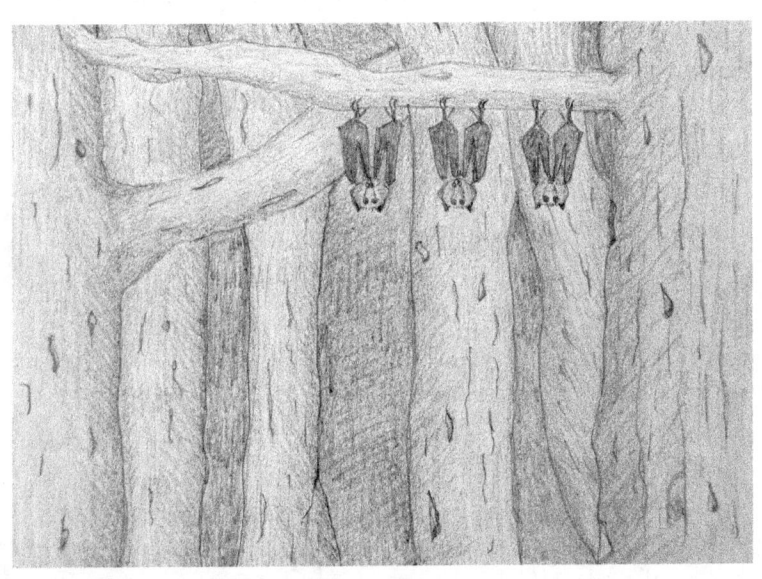

around the outside just to be sure. It had a sweet sourness. She ate half. After a minute she popped more in her mouth, chewing and swallowing in a sweet oblivion.

The bats looked down at her from their barren perch. The trees around were woody and bare. There was no foliage, a desolate enclave. Even the sounds of birds and insects was gone. Its lifelessness suddenly spooked. What is this place, Enoki thought, as the branch of berries fell from her hands. The spook twisted. The woods turned. Its spin made its way to her insides.

An encroaching sickness creeped. A nausea emerged from her stomach to her throat. A shudder of panic and faintness gripped her as she felt beads of sweat accumulate on her brow. The sickness grew. Oh no, she deflected, as her heart sank to the pit of her stomach.

A terrible sinking dragged at her as she doubled over wanting to dry wretch. Perspiration exuded from her skin as she clutched her waist and in a twisted tilt of her head looked up at the bats.

What have you done to me? She garbled. They made a chippering chuckling sound.

You fiends, she hissed.

They had been a deception. They weren't fruit bats. They were vampires. The berries were bait.

She was the meat.

Enoki collapsed to the ground on hands and knees. She crouched into a ball and started to shiver. Her breathing heavied. She thought she was going to die. In and out she breathed. Please, please, please. Then a thousand odes rushed through her head, their iambic crunched to a mono syllable crash.

Out of the corner of her eye she could see the bats fly off, disappearing into the night trailing with a sound like cackling hyenas. What have I done? Enoki thought. This must be some sort of mistake.

Enoki couldn't move. It affected her muscles making them stiff. She just sat crouched on her knees. Her joints creaked like a rusted hinge. She couldn't stay kneeling like this. Her knees started to pain. With one arm stretched out, she rolled onto her side. She curled into a ball and shivered.

She lay low and breathed, counting each minute of breath. Her thoughts raced back to retrace her steps, a new verse of if onlys and why fors. She did not kill to eat. She had no fire to burn. They should have left her alone, these vampires. They picked the wrong meat.

As daylight emerged like splinters through the wood, Enoki rose and swayed to her feet. A new tenseness had descended within her beyond the faded poison.

Be damned these animals, she said to herself through clenched teeth.

She wandered the wood in a daze, checking for vermin in the trees, checking her steps, re-evaluating, calculating, summoning a being greater than her to reveal how this could all come to be. For days she was lost. Unable to walk more than a mile. Hiding in hollows for refuge until they were not. Sleeping covered in leaves. Walking as though in a dream. The terrible ones confused by reality. Congested, unable to erase. Until she walked and walked without her compass, not looking anymore. Not knowing where to go.

Her foot prints upon this ground if you looked behind were like the dents left in dry sand, no shape nor form to reveal the inhabitant of its carriage. Just clefted mounds upon a dimpled dune. In danger of sinking and collapsing with any wrong step. Enoki just walked and walked. This woody cloister with its spear like sticks perverted a straight passage. She carved a different way around the trees, her steps both quickened and dragged, hesitant with every move.

She bit her lip and forged ahead. The vines started to dangle around branches. A leafy density re-emerged in her sight. But it had a swampy thickness. She could only push through. There was no retreat. She waded ahead into its darkness.

Chapter 10

A fine mist cast its breath through a break in the trees. It swirled like a stalking cat around trunks, hesitant on approach, until it hung like a shawl on a broken being. Enoki searched through the thickened haze. There would have to be a point somewhere on the horizon the field of vision would expand, if not for a point in time. The haze would dissipate. Disintegrate before she would. Her vision had become so blurred.

She clasped her eyes shut. All that remained was the air. She could smell the thickness of its scent. Vapour could stifle too. She opened her eyes. She thought she could see an area ahead of her that showed a thinning. She waded forward, until the tempo of her step quickened. Enoki gasped in a half daze, uncertain where she was.

In the mist ahead there appeared to be a white

form moving. Enoki dipped and tilted her head and squinted in curiosity. She rubbed her eyes. Was it just a swirl of fog? She stepped forward, peering in its direction trying to make out what this object was.

A strangeness descended upon the landscape as the fog cleared showing a marshy pond where upon its bank stood a bird. The creature dipped and tilted its head on Enoki's approach. It stopped still. Enoki shifted and braced. She could feel herself hold her breath.

The bird gave her a penetrating stare. Enoki could feel her heart pump. I know who you are, Enoki thought in a slow beating rhythm.

The bird's silence was piercing. Its eyes cast a disconcerting look. The look of judgement. Enoki looked away. But rather than turn her body to run, she looked back at the bird and slowly crouched down upon her knees before it. The iciness of the air cooled her cheeks as her blood beat.

You're not from here, she said quietly out loud to the bird. Maybe you lost your way.

This bird found an oasis in this forest. It found its only means of survival at this pond. It was a water bird, a long way from its sea. A forest to an albatross would be like a desert to a fish. How did an albatross end up in a forest? Picked up and chained by a wind that dragged him to a place not of his

choosing.

But here, by this pond he found his source of water. Here he found a place though he didn't belong. And that look he gave her dictated Enoki did not belong here either. But each did not know the other. Condemned to a place that was not home. A pair of doves who lost their way when released by the hands of their trapper. Enoki slowly raised her head in the ethereal stillness, looking above.

The sky above was framed. The most unusual formation of clouds was moving fast, up high, as though in a hurry toward something. Their backdrop was a still, stagnant grey. The moving clouds were illuminated behind as they hurried through the sky. It was strange. A perverse distortion. She thought it was beautiful.

The beauty in its perversity was to her from its deprivation. The sky was so scarce in Enoki's forest. And a cloud was of a place somewhere else. And a moving cloud was a vision of escape. Its backlit of sun gave it life, devoid of any low. Enoki just stopped and stared. There were few moments in this place where one could see beyond what was right in front.

Can a cloud read your mind, she wondered. They always appeared in a moment of magic. When you looked up and noticed. And would make you feel something, usually tied to their distance from you. These clusters of vapour were a spell. As though you were close enough to breathe in their angel dust. But the folds in an angel's wings revealed grey. Underneath was where Enoki resided. Under their cloudy canopy, was a canopy under another of leaves upon twisted branches. The forest interjected its dominance and asserted Enoki's presence within its forever boundary. The sky was black within its frame. A frame of black silhouette leaves.

Enoki's eyes lowered back to the bird, framed by his pond. Maybe he would disperse like a cloud of vapour. Proving her eyes had blurred in a hallucinating vision too unreal to be believed. Enoki lowered her head, until her chin dipped in defeat. How was she going to get out of here?

Downcast, her ebony eyes matched the blackness of a soul suppressed from a spark to life. It beat slow. Submerged in a mud of inertia. Which way was she supposed to go? She stood up from the bird, who had not moved before her. All she could do was look beyond him. Her eyes wandered heavily ahead, along with a body that followed.

Chapter 11

The rain fell. Enoki stopped and sat, resting her back against the bark of a tree and closed her eyes. With a body too numb to feel, the rain wet her hair, her dress and her face. She was too weary to care. The sound of drops on leaves and bark had collided in her head as a lulling friend and a disruptive foe. As her breathing slowed, a gentle weight had returned. The moth had found his way back and perched like an amulet upon her chest with the rise and fall of its slow syncopating rhythm.

The moth couldn't distinguish whether the drops from above were from Enoki's tears or the rain. No tears fell from Enoki's eyes. She was too tired to cry. A thousand tears fell from the sky that Enoki could not shed.

Enoki had been in this forest for a thousand days. If she survived a thousand days she could survive a thousand more. The forest was a duration. It had a shrinkage on her being from the oppressive force of it's never. In this moment, her only stability was here at the base of a tree. Its strength in stature was the only structure above a foundation of earth capable of withstanding the weight of Enoki's soul. Anything else in this forest was wisp and flimsy or sliced and ripped and tore.

The night fell along with the rain. The darkness hid Enoki and the moth as she cradled at the base of the tree. If a raindrop could transform into a star, she'd throw their water back to the sky. So much rain had wet her skin, if she could flick them back to the sky as stars, there would be no clouds to rain upon her again, only lights that sparkle.

At dawn, Enoki opened her eyes. She pulled her body up from the ground. The moth fluttered up and around making his way to the back of her shoulder.

She looked around to gain her bearings. The area was dense with trees shrouded with tangled vines like boas. It surrounded a small arbour of open ground. It wasn't until she turned around that she made sight of the tree that she had rested on for the night. She stepped back with the vision of its enormity. Its trunk was thick and wide which carried branches that splayed spectacularly either side creating a canopy like the roof of a pavilion.

ENOKI

She stepped back further to admire it in awe. She hadn't seen any other tree like it through the entirety of this forest. She didn't know what type of tree it was. It had a bark that was solid to the touch and a hollow up and to its side where she could see copper sap bleed. Its leaves waxy and firm. Its branches both raised and hugged.

If Enoki had been in a game and X marked the spot where you had reached its pinnacle point, she hoped it marked its final threshold.

Please tell me you're a sign that home is on the other side, she said.

She took in a moment to breathe in its splendour. But she knew nature was made up of aberrant circles. The first glimpse of this tree encouraged the thought that she was indeed walking through and not around within. If this was a symbol she hoped it was not its centre, but where the forest marked its hieroglyph like a buoy in a sea. An object close to the edge that marked a relief. Maybe Enoki would soon reach her shore.

She stared at the tree in wonder. What if it grew from the bones of a man that got close to the edge, but couldn't see a relief in sight. Here he stopped, unable to continue. Here his bones scarred the earth upon which this new life grew. A proof of life. Its ascendancy was able to reach the ultimate view.

A place he failed to see. A view to the other side. To the end of the forest. Here it projected the point of liberty. The forest was its price.

Enoki could feel the weight of the moth upon her, like the hand of another human, bearing witness beside her. She turned her head back to him momentarily, before looking back to the tree. It was then that she saw its patience. The tree had been waiting for her to find it.

If only its bark could be read like a map where she could trace the curves to a border. But if it were, its map would never remain the same. It was always shifting, expanding. Then she noticed its bark was shedding its skin like a cicada. In a silent profound expression. Unlike any human. She looked down at her hands, with their lines and cracks and crevices. She'd carry their weather like a cameo. Her feet would carry the stains of the same earth upon which this tree stood. Time had stamped upon her. A time she could not shed.

By days end a sunset burned red in reflection as it pressed itself against the bark of the tree. The moth flew up from her shoulder resting on the trunk of the tree. It was then Enoki knew it was time to go.

Chapter 12

Agentle breeze twirled around the wood softly striking Enoki's hair. The air had a lightness. The scent of heavy earth lifted as Enoki stepped forward into an everglade that opened to a view of the entire sky, framed by a shawl of leaves. A kiss from the moon made the leaves glisten like stars in Enoki's night. She looked ahead. Before her was a scene unbelievable to Enoki's eyes.

In the distance she could see what looked like a city. There appeared a stack of buildings illumined like a clutch of lighthouses. Their tiny windows dotted with lights within their frames. Enoki dropped to her knees and stared. The stars above them shrieked like exploding thistles. But it was the buildings that held the life with light only from human hands. Someone had struck the switch that lit the room. Within one would be an abode with a

ENOKI

bed. Within was another being within four walls that was theirs alone. Within was a home.

Enoki looked down to see the space in between her and the towers. Below was a flat dense valley. It looked a distance possible to traverse. It was a distance far shorter than the one from which she had come. She could sense the beating within her chest rise in longing. If she could unravel it like a pin-pricked scroll its imprint would cast a trillion steps. The trace of this forest's contest. A track of endurance.

Here, an end to the forest was before her. It was the border she was seeking. Now she knelt upon this precipice. She looked ahead into the night sky. She wanted to find that cerulean blue. She could stay where she was for the night, wait for the sunrise, wait for the sky to show its hue.

But to wait was to starve.

Enoki looked back to the forest, behind her into its midnight ink. She face forward to the lights ahead, cradled by the edge of the forest. To look back was to look forward. Where she would go mattered less than from where she had come. She understood this forest's past. She understood its path. Its ridges, its corners, its curves and projections. There had only ever been one way. The way that breaches the deepest point before the break of a wave. The only way was through.

ENOKI

ANNA.M.L

Acknowledgements

The wave rockwall illustration inspired by images of the rock formation known as The Wave located in Western Australia.

Forest dragon illustration inspired by the photography of Mike Prociv, Australian Geographic, Issue 69, Jan-Mar 2003.

Albatross illustration inspired by the photography of Aaron Russ, Australian Geographic, Issue 77, Jan-Mar 2005.

Arendt, Hannah. *The Human Condition*, 1958. Second Edition, University of Chicago Press, 2018.

www.ingramcontent.com/pod-product-compliance
Lightning Source LLC
Chambersburg PA
CBHW070637120726
47909CB00004B/1467